HOW HUNGRY ARE YOU?

For Robert, who saw a better way.
—D. J. N. and R. T.

To my wonderful friend Rebecca, who
loves picnics and is good at sharing, and
special thanks to my furry and feathered
friends at 10 Mellen Street.

—A. W.

Atheneum Books for Young Readers
An imprint of Simon & Schuster Children's Publishing Division
1230 Avenue of the Americas
New York, New York 10020

Book design by Angela Carlino
The text of this book is set in Ad Lib.
The illustrations are rendered in cut-paper.

Printed in Hong Kong NOV 2 0 2001

10 9 8 7 6 5 4 3 2 1

Library of Congress Cataloging-in-Publication Data
Napoli, Donna Jo, 1948-
How hungry are you? / by Donna Jo Napoli and Richard Tchen ;
illustrated by Amy Walrod.
p.   cm.
Summary: An ever-increasing group of children go on a picnic,
finding a way to divide the food that they all have contributed.
ISBN 0-689-83389-X
[1. Picnicking—Fiction. 2. Division—Fiction. 3. Sharing—Fiction.]
I. Tchen, Richard. II. Walrod, Amy, ill. III. Title.

PZ7.N15 Ho 2001
[E]—dc21   00-042020

FIRST
EDITION

HOW HUNGRY ARE YOU?

written by **Donna Jo Napoli** and **Richard Tchen**

illustrated by **Amy Walrod**

Atheneum Books for Young Readers
New York London Toronto Sydney Singapore

"I'm hungry."

 "Want to go on a picnic?"

 "Sure."

 "I'll make sandwiches if you bring bug juice. How hungry are you?"

 "HUNGRY."

"Twelve sandwiches. Does that sound like enough for the two of us?"

 "Hmmm. Okay."

R'S MAGIC BOLOGNA

poof

12 SLICES

SPICY
MUSTARD

 mayonnaise

"Where are you going, guys?"

 "On a picnic."

 "Can I come?"

 "Can she come?"

 "Only if she brings food."

 "What have you got to eat?"

 "My mom just made cookies. I could take a dozen."

 "Four sandwiches each and four cookies each. What do you say?"

 "Yum."

"What's up?"

 "We're going on a picnic."

 "Can I come?"

 "Can she come?"

 "Another girl? Well, what's she got to eat?"

 "What's she got to eat?"

 "What have you got to eat?"

 "Rice pudding packs."

 "How many?"

 "Twelve."

 "Three sandwiches, three cookies, and three rice pudding packs each. What do you say?"

 "Yum, yum."

 "Is food all you guys think about?"

"Hey, is this a party or something?"

 "Yeah, is this a party?"

 "We're going on a picnic."

 "Oh, no, it's the twins."

 "They always have gum. Ask them if they have gum."

 "Do you have gum?"

 "Yeah."

 "Yeah."

 "How much?"

 "Twelve sticks."

 "Yeah, twelve."

 "Chewing gum or bubble gum?"

 "Chewing gum."

 "Yeah, chewing gum."

 "Go home."

"But they're really good flavors."

 "Yeah, good."

 "What flavors?"

 "Variety."

 "Yeah, all sorts."

 "Yay. I get banana."

 "Two of everything for each of us."

 "We better run the rest of the way."

"Hold up. Why's everyone running?"

 "We're going on a picnic. And there's six
of you, so you can't come."

 "Who cares? We're going to the park.
And we've got watermelon."

 "Watermelon? Did you say watermelon?
I love watermelon! Hey you, is the rice
pudding watermelon flavor?"

 "Are you nuts? Rice pudding is never watermelon flavor."

 "Hey, you two, is any of the chewing gum watermelon flavor?"

 "No."

 "Yeah, no."

 "Hey, you, with the cookies . . ."

"Oh, never mind. I've got to have watermelon."

 "How many pieces do you have?"

 "Twelve."

 "That's one each."

 "But if we don't share with you guys, we get two each."

 "But if you do share, you get a sandwich and a cookie and a rice pudding pack and chewing gum."

 "We're coming."

 "Stop talking and run."

"We made it."

"Let's spread everything out."

"Look how pretty that is."

"Hi, everyone. A picnic. Can I join?"

 "No."

 "Go away."

 "Yeah, go away."

 "What have you got to eat?"

 "You can't ask him that. He makes thirteen. We've only got twelve of everything."

 "I don't have anything. I'll just watch you eat."

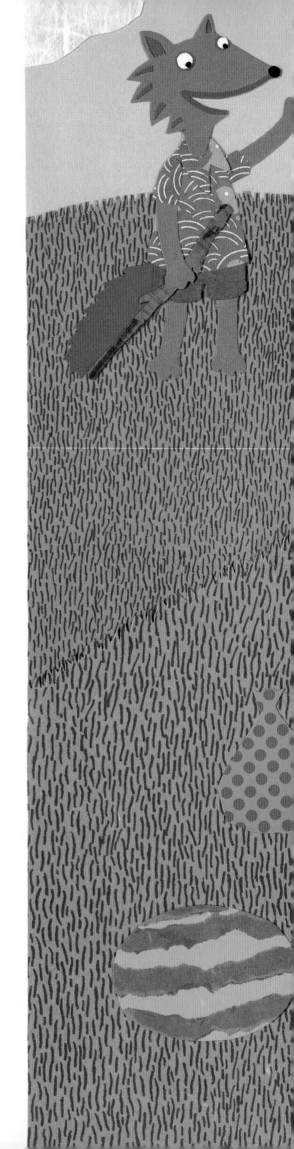

 "Oh."

 "It looks good."

 "That's not nice."

 "It smells good."

 "Go home."

 "Yeah, go home."

 "I love watermelon."

 "Did you have to say that? Now, did you have to say that? That's not fair. I don't want to feel sorry for you, and I'm hungrier than ever now!"

 "I really love watermelon."

"That's it. We've got to share."

 "But you're the one who said you were
  hungry."

 "We share."

 "How?"

 "I have an idea. Everyone can have a
  sandwich except me. And I get everything
  else."

 "No."

 "Yeah, no."

"Then everyone except me can have one of each thing but I get a bite of everyone else's."

 "Nu-uh. You take giant bites."

 "How about we all walk back ten feet, then at the count of three, we can race for the food we like best?"

 "That's stupid."

 "I'm hungry."

 "All right, let's eat."

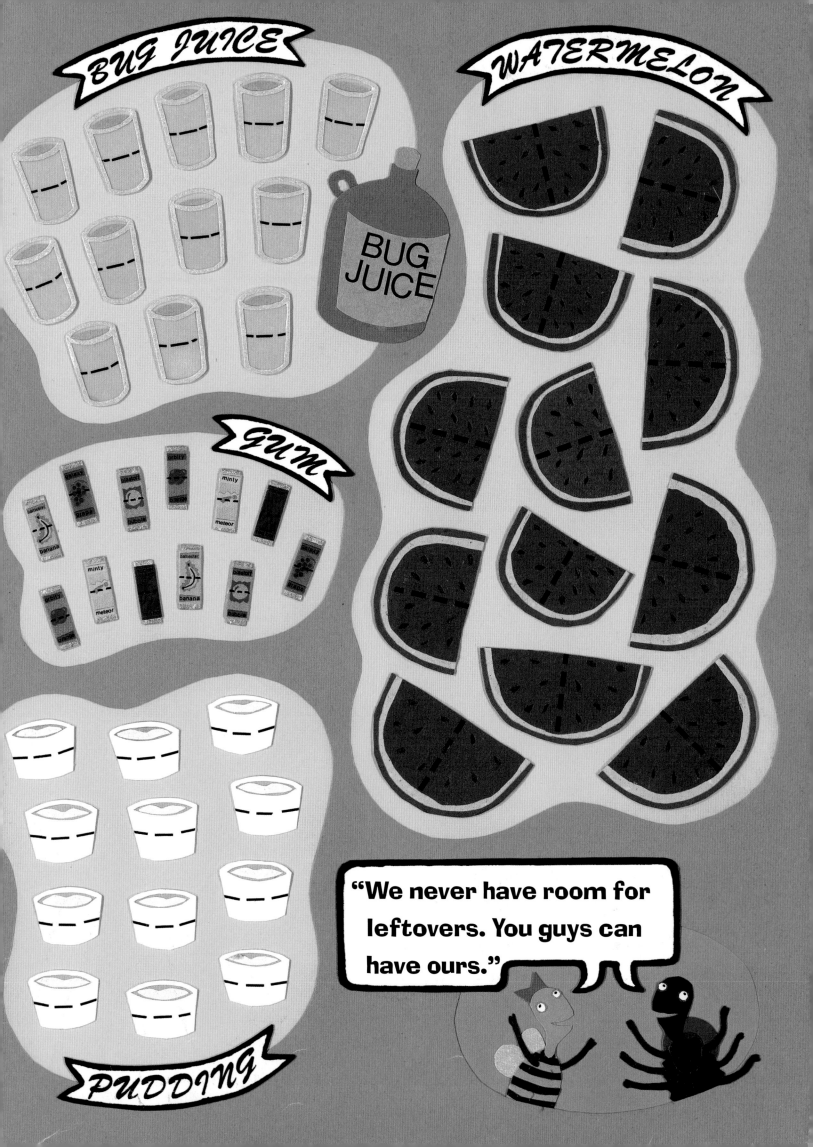

"That sounds nice."

 "Yeah, civilized."

 "Well, then, I call the second half of the banana chewing gum."

 "Don't talk with your mouth full."